MARKED BY FATE

SARAH K L WILSON

SEVENTEEN-YEAR-OLD ZOE MUST DEVISE A KICKASS PLAN TO THWART EVIL
OR WATCH THE WORLD BURN.

SWORDS & STILETTOS

KRISTIN D VAN RISSEGHEM

ALLIE HAS ALWAYS BELIEVED LIFE IS SIMPLE.
YOU'RE BORN. YOU LIVE. YOU DIE.
BUT HER AWAKENING IS ABOUT TO SHOW HER HOW THOSE THOSE RULES HAVE EVER
APPLIED TO HER.

MELISSA A CRAVEN

INCREDIBLE POWERS. A WORLD IN DANGER.
ONE GIRL WILL SAVE OR END HUMANITY.

MIDNIGHT SOCIETY

RHONDA SERMON

FANTASY OF FROST

KELLY ST CLARE

CURSE OF THE SPHINX

RAYE WAGNER

EDNAH WALTERS

Illustrated by
ARNILD ALDEPOLLA

THERE ARE THREE KINDS OF MAGIC IN THE WORLD,
AND CORENTINE HAS THE WRONG ONE.

SHIFT OF SHADOW & SOUL

HILLARY THOMPSON

FATE BROUGHT HER PEOPLE TO EARTH,
NOW IT'S MARKED FOR DEATH.

FATE'S LEGACY

ANGELA FRISTOE

THREE SISTERS. ONE DESTINY. WRONG WORLD.
ANA IS BECOMING THE SAVIOR THE WORLD NEEDS,
ONLY SHE'S IN THE WRONG DIMENSION.

BECOMING :
THE BALANCE
BRINGER

DEBRA KRISTI

Believe and become your potential

BOUND TOGETHER.
WORLDS APART.

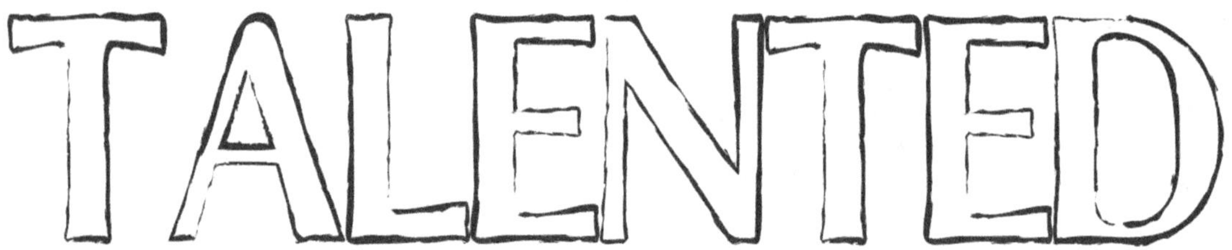

SIOBHAN DAVIS

THREE WORLDS. ONE RULE.
SHE MUST NEVER OPEN A DOOR.

DOORMAKER: ROCK OF HEAVEN

Jamie Thornton

LITA DIDN'T EXPECT TO INHERIT TROUBLE
WHEN HER ECCENTRIC UNCLE DIED.

HOW TO TALK TO GHOSTS

ERIN HAYES

FOLLOW YOUR HEART

WHAT IF YOU COULD GO BACK IN TIME TO SAVE THE PERSON YOU LOVE THE MOST?

THE CLAY LION

AMALIE JAHN

A GIRL, A PROPHECY, AND TWO WARRING GODS
EQUALS DESTINY!

THE HEALER

C J ANAYA

MURDEROUS GNOMES? HUNGRY TROLLS? DEATH MATCH AGAISNT AN EVIL SORCERESS?
YESTERDAY VAN'S ONLY CONCERN WAS PASSING FINALS.

D DL LARMILLEI

VIKKA IS FORCED TO SELL HER ORGANS TO PAY HER FAMILY'S OXYGEN BILL, BUT A CHANCE ENCOUNTER WITH A RICH BOY WILL CHANGE HER LIFE FOREVER.

JACKSON DEAN CHASE

LOLA'S NOT PRETTY. LOLA'S NOT POPULAR.
LOLA WISHES SHE COULD DISAPPEAR … AND THEN ONE DAY SHE DOES JUST THAT…

INVISIBLE

JEANNE BANNON

Copyright: blackspring / 123RF Stock Photo

HER ELDERS STILL TELL HER WHAT TO DO, AND HER GRASP OF REALMISTRY IS AVERAGE AT BEST, SO HOW'SBRONWYN SUPPOSED TO STOP THE GORMON INVASION AND THE DEATH OF EVERYONE SHE LOVES?.

SHADOWS OF THE REALM

DIONNE LISTER

SANCTUARY

MELLE AMADE

MEADOW'S PSYCHIC POWERS RUINED HER LIFE ONCE. NOW THEY'RE BACK AND JUST AS BENT
ON DESTROYING HER AS BEFORE.

INGRID SEYMOUR

Meadow

LENA MAE HILL

TRIALS OF A TEENAGE WEREVULTURE

EMILY MARTHA SORENSEN

SHE POSSESSES A GIFT PUNISHABLE BY DEATH. HE IS A SPY FOR HIS POWERFUL SCOTTISH CLAN. NOTHING ABOUT THIS RELATIONSHIP IS GOING TO BE EASY.

THE EDINBURGH SEER

ALISHA KLAPHEKE

MAGIC AWAKENED: MORGANA CHRONICLES BOOK ONE

MEG COWLEY

Meg Cowley
www.megcowley.com

WE HOPE YOU'VE ENJOYED THE MARKED BY FATE COLORING BOOK

Visit us at MarkedByFate.com to learn more
about the books featured in our upcoming boxset

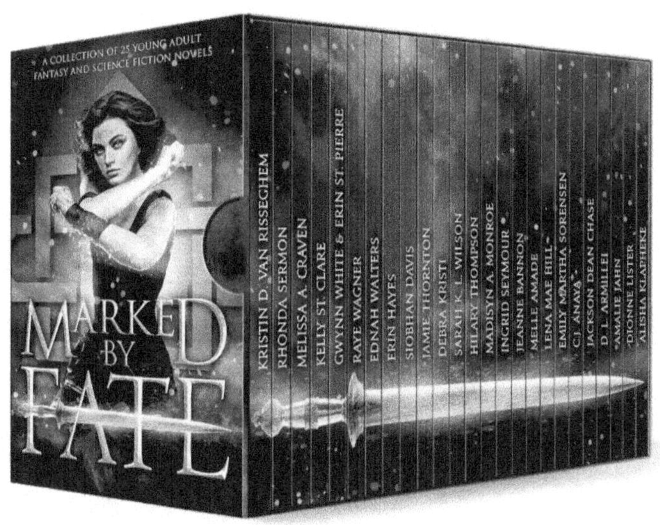

Marked by Fate is available on these formats:
Amazon | iBooks | Nook | Kobo | Google Play

Follow us on
Facebook: @markedbyfate
Twitter: @MarkedByF8
Instagram: @markedbyfatehq

And check out our giveaways at MarkedByFate.com